Moving Gives Me A Stomach Ache

© Copyright 1988
Text by Heather McKend,
Illustrations by Heather Collins
Design by Glyphics Inc

Published in September 1988 by:

Black Moss Press
P.O. Box 143, Station A
Windsor, Ontario N9A 6L7
Canada

with the assistance of the Canada
Council and the Ontario Arts
Council.

Black Moss Press Books are
distributed in Canada and the
United States by:

Firefly Books
3520 Pharmacy Avenue
Unit 1-C
Scarborough, Ontario M1W 2T8
Canada.

All orders should be directed there.

ISBN 0-88753-178-4
First printing September 1988.

Printed in Canada by
The National Press, Toronto, Ontario.

M O V I N G
GIVES ME A STOMACH ACHE

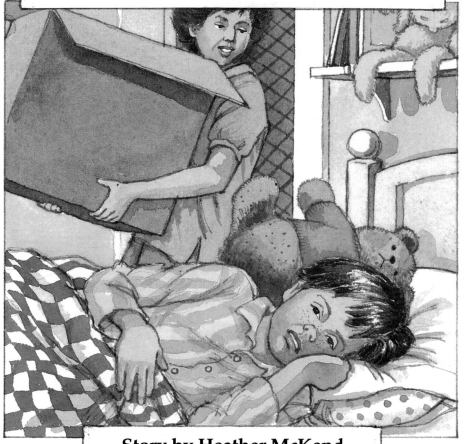

Story by Heather McKend
Illustrations by Heather Collins

Black Moss Press 1988

When I woke up it was raining.

Maybe the house is crying because we're moving today.

I think I have a stomach ache because we're moving today.

You really shouldn't make a guy move when he has a stomach ache.

My Mom gave me
one big box and
told me to put in
anything I wanted
to take to the new
house.

I looked outside at my soggy climbing tree.

I looked at the big box. You can't fit a tree in one little box.

It's funny how big boxes can suddenly get little.

I said I need a bigger box
because I want to take my tree.

Nobody was listening

I said louder could
I have a bigger box
or two smaller boxes
because I NEED
to take my tree.

I said my tree wants
to come and if I can't
take my tree I think
I will throw up.

My mother said to stop being silly and pack.

So I got my best and most important stuff out from under my bed where I always keep it until Mom finds it.

I got out my Baby's ABC Book which is perfect except for the missing Z page.

Who uses Z besides Zebras anyway?

I packed Mom's ring box where I keep my dead pet bee, George.

I packed my one
old running shoe.
A guy never knows
when he'll need
another shoe.

I didn't HAVE to
take my bear, but
he likes to travel.

Then I packed my 34 marbles, 3 checkers, a real pretend sports car, a borrowed pot lid I guess I forgot to unborrow and a melted chocolate bar I've been saving. A guy never knows when he's going to get hungry.

But the box was almost full so I figured I'd better eat the chocolate to make more room.

My stomach felt worse but there still wasn't enough room to fit in my best friend Pinkie.

....Or my tree.

I thought Pinkie might fit in the box if I could fold him.

But I accidently folded his leg
the wrong way and he said
it hurt and kicked me and said
he wasn't my friend anymore
and went home.

I said that was fine with me
because I didn't want to pack
him anyway.

I couldn't take my stuffed parrot with one diamond eye so I sold it to Frances for 27¢.

I figured I could use 27¢ for bus fare to get back here after we moved. I was going to go back for my tree.

My Mom put my box in the car and said it was time to go.

I looked back at our crying
house and tree but my eyes
felt blurry and my stomach
did too.

Mom said the new family
would take care of
everything.

She hugged me
and I fell asleep.

When I woke up we were at the new house. It was sunny. Maybe the lonely new house was smiling to see us.

I looked in the backyard and found a tree. Not as good as my old tree but it would do until I had enough money for bus fare.

Mom says there's a kid next door. Not as good as my best friend Pinkie but he'll do as second best friend.

I still don't like moving. It's hard on a guy.

But after you finish moving, your stomach ache goes away.